FRIDAY NIGHT AT

Hodges' Cafe

WRITTEN AND ILLUSTRATED BY

TIM EGAN

Houghton Mifflin Company
Boston 1994

For Ann, My Love.

Library of Congress Cataloging-in-Publication Data

Egan, Tim.
    Friday night at Hodges' cafe / Tim Egan.
    p.   cm.
    Summary: Hodges and the patrons of his cafe are frightened when
three tigers try to take over, but his crazy duck saves the day.
    ISBN 0-395-68076-X
    [1. Tigers—Fiction.   2. Ducks—Fiction.   3. Restaurants—
Fiction.]   I. Title.
PZ7.E2815Fr   1994   93-11290
[E]—dc20   CIP
                             AC

Printed in the United States of America

BVG   10   9   8   7   6   5   4   3   2   1

HODGES' CAFE was busy as usual last Friday night. Everyone was savoring the delicious desserts that the cafe is famous for. Hodges is considered by many to be the finest pastry chef in the city.

Too bad his duck is so crazy.

Everybody likes the duck. He's just a little different. Sometimes he throws ice cream on the floor just to watch it smoosh. He's also been known to dive into raspberry tarts, and, on occasion, he kicks strawberries

across the room. Hodges, who is otherwise very calm
and patient, gets upset every time and always makes
the duck clean up the mess.

But everyone knows it will happen again.

Anyway, last Friday night the customers seemed to be enjoying themselves when the door suddenly flew open and a cold breeze came whistling in. Along with the breeze came three big, hungry tigers dressed in rather expensive looking clothes.

Everyone fell silent except for the duck.

"Gee, they must not have seen the 'No Tigers' sign on the door right in front of their faces," the duck said loudly, proving he really was crazy.

The tigers just sneered at him.

They sat down at a table in the corner. The one holding the cane looked at Hodges and said, "I believe my palate is in dire need of some exotic delicacy. Perhaps Elephant Schnitzel would satisfy my appetite. Hmm, hmm."

Everyone was petrified.

But the duck said, "We don't serve that here. Didn't you read the menu?"

The tiger jumped at the duck, but the duck was
ready for him. He kicked an almond torte that hit
the tiger right in the face and sent him falling back
into his chair.

There was a hush over the room.

Then the tiger with the gold suspenders looked over at Stan, the pig, and said, "Tsk, tsk. My taste buds require something even more refined and tantalizing. I think Pigs Benedict, lightly salted, is my dish of choice."

"We don't serve that here either," explained the duck. "Maybe you should try another restaurant."

The tiger growled menacingly and started toward the duck.

The duck calmly picked up a tray of caramel custards and threw them at the tiger's feet. The tiger slipped on them and went crashing to the floor.

Then the biggest tiger stood up and snarled, "It is my considered opinion that the most flavorful entrée of all would be Sautéed Duck in an orange glaze."

All at once, the tigers were wildly chasing the crazy
duck all over the restaurant. Some of his friends tried

to help by throwing cheesecakes and rhubarb pies at the tigers, but most of them weren't very good shots.

Things got a little out of control.

Suddenly the biggest tiger caught the duck. They
looked each other straight in the eye. No one moved.

It was a tense moment.

All this time, Hodges hadn't said a word. He seemed as calm as always. But then, without warning, he picked up a chocolate soufflé and shoved it into the biggest tiger's face.

No one could believe it.

The tiger dropped the duck, who quickly dove into a large raspberry tart. All three tigers showed their big, sharp teeth and terrifying claws. They seemed very upset and about to do something dangerous.

Then the biggest tiger paused and said, "Wait a minute."
He licked his paw and declared, "This is without a doubt
the most exquisite soufflé I have ever had the pleasure of
experiencing. It is magnificent."

With that, the duck stuck his head out of the tart and said, "Well, you should try the lemon meringue pie."

Then the crazy duck laughed nervously, jumped up,
and started dancing around on the counter, singing:

"I like cakes and I like pies,
I like sweets that are twice my size."

It was hard not to laugh, so everybody did.

Well, the tigers didn't really laugh, but they smiled, sort of. They certainly seemed impressed with Hodges' incredible food.

One of them said,
"We'll take three of your
finest Boston cream pies,
if you please."

"Will that be to go or to
eat here?" asked Hodges.

The tigers looked at one another.

"My colleagues and I would prefer to delight in these richly resplendent pies in the comfort of your simple yet dignified establishment," said the one with the cane.

"You mean you want to eat them here?" Hodges asked.

"Precisely," replied the tiger.

So they stayed and ate, and everyone talked. It was
a little hard to understand what the tigers were saying
because they talked so fancy, but they seemed much

friendlier. The duck even made them laugh once.

All things considered, it turned out to be a fairly
nice evening.

And later that night, after everyone left, Hodges
took the "No Tigers" sign off the door.